I0688563

A Rough Season

Second Edition

L.L. Angelo

A Rough Season

Second edition
Radical Bookshop and Press
4838 Richard Road SW, Suite 300
Calgary, AB T3E 6L1

FIC029000 – Fiction, Short Stories

First edition published by:
Loft 112
#112, 535 8 Avenue SE
Calgary, AB Canada T2G 5S9

Inner City Stories
Volume 21
January 17, 2020

Editors: Sabrina Uswak and Silvia Pikal

First edition cover design: Stacey Walyuchow
Second edition cover design: L.L. Angelo

ISBN-13: 978-1-988712-49-9 (eBook)

ISBN-13: 978-1-7770865-1-0

Printed in Canada

For Ryan

Contents

CHAPTER 1

Calling...

Hey Rory, how are you buddy? Yeah, I'm up in Fort Mac tomorrow. Ten days on. Four off. Yeah man, going back to camp to freeze my balls off. Colder than a witch's tit. Amy keeps telling me to get a job downtown but I'm making seventy-five an hour on the rigs. That's good fucking money. I told Max I could get him up there. Nah, don't listen to his shit, he's not a foreman. No, he's not. He's just some Timmy's bitch with an orange vest. Ten and four is a money shift. I'm already eyeing up a new Tacoma. Black with black interior. Gonna be pimp.

Where are you watching the game tonight? The Ship? Monahan is out with a groin injury — again. Fuck, I hate watching us get shit-kicked by the Leafs. Did you see that goal on Smith last night? Backhand top shelf? Jesus boys. Where was the defence on that? Lucky that

Johnny sniped one from the point to tie it up but we shit the bed in overtime like we always do. We're never gonna make it with single-pointers. Yeah, I'll come out for a few but then I gotta head'er and pack. We still on for the long weekend? Sweet. I just picked up my board. She's waxed and ready. I hope you're picking us up because Max hates when I drive. Guy is such a dumb-ass. Last time we were up at Louise, he yard-saled off a cliff and dislocated his shoulder. Don't hit it if you can't commit it, man. Anyway, gimme fifteen to warm up the honey-hauler and I'll meet you there.'

CHAPTER 2

The Ship & Anchor

Snow was coming down thick and 17th Avenue was a nightmare of parked cars pushed against dirty snowbanks. Outside, Drew passed a group of girls wearing skirts and high heels. No wonder chicks are always so cold. Drew pushed past them. A guard stood sentinel at the doors, a thick-necked man who kept tally of people going in and out. Drew rubbed his palms together as he entered the pub and waded into a sea of toques and hockey jerseys. The walls were painted kale green, scuffed with wood-paneling up to the chair rail. Flags were pinned to the ceiling next to jerseys from Arsenal, Chelsea and Real Madrid. Two bartenders were operating on auto-pilot; checking drink tickets spitting from the machine and ignoring assholes shouting orders from the crowd.

'There's never any parking around here,' said Drew as he grabbed a barstool and nudged himself next to his buddy Rory. Max was already there. Drew elbowed a bit of room at the high-top table and pushed Max further into the corner. 'What's the score?'

'Still nothing in the first,' said Rory. He had on his usual plaid jacket. His iPhone was face-up on the table and his girlfriend Jessica was calling but he didn't notice. Drew thought about saying something but —*And it's a battle for the puck in the corner, Ferland checks Komarov — the puck is loose and picked up by Bennet who gets a shot away.* Every eye was glued to the white-blue glow of the television screen as it illuminated faces and cast shadows over the half-empty pints and bones of chicken wings.

'Do we have a server?' asked Drew glancing over his shoulder.

'Yeah but it's friggin' packed in here. I think she's at the bar waiting for our next round,' said Rory as he craned his neck around the crowd.

The servers stood in a gaggle at the corner of the bar. A brunette was tugging at her mini-kilt uniform. A wave of steam gushed from the dishwasher and the bartenders unloaded a fresh stock of glasses. The kilted servers arranged circles of drinks around baskets of pulled pork poutines coming too quickly out of the kitchen. *Giordano dumps the puck deep into the Leafs' zone as the penalty to Brodie ends. Both teams head off to the bench to make a change.*

'Atta boy, Gio!' Max bellowed.

'You know there's free parking on second street — behind the gay bathhouse,' said Rory casually. He took a sip of his beer.

'What gay bathhouse?' Drew skewed his face.

'The one next to that hipster restaurant. It's a random door but my buddy's been inside — he's a firefighter. Dudes get their dicks so steamed up that the alarms go off and the fire department has to shut it down. You can see the steam coming out of the roof.'

'Dude, that's sick,' said Max shaking his head.

'I don't care about that shit. Free parking is free parking.'

'Can I get you anything?' A semi-attractive server appeared. Her waist was small but her crooked eyes bulged out of her lids. She set two full pints on the table and two more plates of wings.

'Yeah, what's on tap?' Drew asked.

'Village Blonde, Wildrose — We've got Velvet Fog and Wraspberry, and um —Alley Kat, Trad, Blue Buck and Jerkface 9000."

'I'll take a Jerkface and ten salt and pepper.'

The bug-eyed girl memorized the order and pushed her way through to the next table.

'There's too many dudes in here and not enough chicks,' said Max taking a sip of his fresh beer and pushing his empty glass to the centre of the table. A pimple-faced dishpig came by and loaded the empties into a grey bin.

'Shit, I missed a call from Jessica,' said Rory looking at his phone.

'How's that going anyway?' asked Drew.

'Yeah, it's fine. She hates that I'm working so much. I think she wants to break up with me—'

Face-off won by the Leafs and there's a long shot by Kadri —REBOUND.

Drew could relate. He broke things off with Amy because she never stopped complaining about his work schedule. What was he supposed to do? That's just how it was up north —long weeks away in exchange for a big fat bank account. Besides, she didn't complain when he paid for dinner or took her away for weekends in Jasper. It didn't matter. He needed to find someone who could deal with the fact that he worked hard, went for beers with the guys and didn't talk about marriage, or kids, or buying a bungalow in Cougar Ridge. *Gaudreau banks it ahead to Tkachuk, tipped it in for Backlund — Tkachuk comes out from behind the net, gets the pass and — SCORES!*

The pub erupted. In the corner of the bar a red light was spinning and a horn blared signaling a first period goal.

'Fuckin' rights, boys! Get up early. Watch the replay on that,' said Rory high-fiving Drew and Max.

And that's a real smart play by Gaudreau... nice little pass to Backlund right on the stick — tape-to-tape — that allows Tkachuk time to get in front and get one past the net minder.

'Beauty—' said Max watching the goal again in slow-motion.

The server brought Drew his order and she took another round of drink requests for the table. Rory switched from beer to double rye and cokes. Max joked about ordering a margarita. 'It a chick-magnet, I swear.'

'Think we'll trade Frolík at the deadline?'

Rory's iPhone vibrated and two kiss emojis appeared on the screen.

'Nah, we won't get shit for him. We should have traded him last season for a second-rounder.' Rory typed a reply to Jessica as Drew checked his email for the third time. Nothing.

14

'What time is your flight up tomorrow?' asked Max.

'I should be on the six-thirty but I'm still waiting on confirmation. Some corporate guy let his daughter manage the crew bookings this month and she always forgets to send the flight confirmations. She just takes selfies all day for Instagram or Snapchat, or whatever the fuck these young chicks are into now.'

'See, this is exactly why I don't work up on the rigs — they just turn you into a grumpy old bastard,' said Max laughing. He punched Drew on the shoulder in a brotherly way but Drew didn't laugh.

'Max — at least you'd be a rich bastard. You're just a piss ant.'

'Who cares? I'm home by five and I don't have to shower with a bunch of ball sacks.'

Drew locked his eyes on the TV. The night before he left was always the worst. Ten days on. That's it man. And when you get back, don't text Amy.

Last month, Drew caved in and they hooked up for a night but the next morning he felt horrible. It didn't help that she thought it was a sign they were getting back together. He was just so lonely and exhausted. At least if Max came up to work with him, they could have dinner together and watch the game. It wouldn't feel so depressing. But there was no point in being sad over what happened with Amy. He wasn't going to be some office robot who walked around with a fake smile and typed passive-aggressive emails to dipshits with too many degrees. That kind of work was for morons. He needed to be doing something real, even if it meant sacrificing things, right? Even if it meant being lonely and dead tired. That's what real work was. *The whistle blows and a penalty is called on defenceman Dougie Hamilton for high-sticking.*

Not a smart play by Hamilton. There's a chance here for the Leafs to tie it up in the final two minutes of the opening act.

'I'm going out for a dart; can you order me another one when the waitress comes back?'

Drew patted himself down looking for a lighter and his cigarettes. He smoked Belmonts now and he wasn't interested in giving them up.

CHAPTER 3

Les Habitants

The ten days up north dragged on like a special kind of hell. Drew ate dinner at camp every night except once when a rookie electrician asked him to go for steak. He was some idiot liberal from Etobicoke who was cracking under the pressure of being isolated at his first work camp. He complained about taking the bus to site at five-thirty in the morning while it was still black as night. Talking to him was nauseating. But Drew made it — again. He was sitting on the plane, one leg extended into the aisle, drinking black coffee with his tray table down. He was going over a checklist of what he needed to pack for the snowboard trip he had the next day. The forecast looked sweet; twenty-two centimetres overnight. He thought about what to do when he landed. A quick shower, text Rory or Max, maybe they could meet for a pint, and then laundry and — don't text Amy. Remember what happened last time? Drew rubbed his palms together. The plane was vibrating and all around him guys were on their laptops, skyping with their wives over the free Wi-Fi. They landed just after lunch and Drew picked up a double-double and an everything bagel with cream cheese before catching a taxi back to his apartment. Even though he was only gone for two weeks, it seemed like little things in his neighbourhood would change. The road construction barrier on 12th Street was gone. A new pizza place opened. The graffiti on the outside of his condo was worse and someone put a new plant in the lobby. Inside his apartment, everything looked stale and untouched. He tossed a loaf of bread in the trash along with two bruised apples. He opened the fridge and surveyed a selection of expired salad dressing and three lonely beers. He cracked a bottle of Kokanee and tossed the metal cap on the counter. His phone buzzed.

— Max: Can't tonight, it's my sister's birthday. We're going to that Mexican place with pineapple tacos.

— Drew: What is with girls and pineapple?

— Max: I know right. See u tomorrow, Rory picking us up?

— Drew: Yeah, ready at seven

— Max: kk

Drew tossed his phone on the couch and decided to take his beer into the shower with him. Max was out. Maybe Rory could meet up. He turned the shower on hot and scrubbed the grease and grit from his body, taking an extra-long time, gulping his beer down in thick swallows as the soap bubbles trailed down his abs. His legs were sore. His back was killing him. How much longer could he do this for? His palms were so calloused they felt like hockey gloves. He turned off the water, wrapped himself in a towel and went into his bedroom. He stood for a moment soaking in the view of the downtown skyline. He was on the fourteenth floor and the view from his beltline apartment pointed directly East at the tall office towers. He turned away and faced the 75-inch flat screen mounted on the wall. Maybe it was a waste of money paying that designer chick to pick out curtains and chairs and fancy rugs, but his place looked money now and she was smokin' hot so how could he say no? He'd had a good night with whatever her name was...Emily? Emma? It was all before Amy entered the picture. Fuck, Amy. Why was he still thinking about her? Drew tried to shake her image from his head. He went back into the living room, grabbed his laptop and jerked off to some porn. He felt shitty about it but he didn't want to slip up and send her a message. She'd want to get back together and then he'd just be that asshole who made a booty call and then took-off for three days to go boarding with his friends.

— Rory: Sorry man, I can't...working late tonight then Jessica is coming over. See u in the morning.

— Drew: Yeah, for sure

Drew pulled on a pair of jeans and a t-shirt and slumped back down on the couch. He turned on the TV and decided to give it an hour before going out alone. The Habs game was just starting. *Welcome to the Barclays Centre where*

Drew heard his phone buzz. He picked it up thinking it might be Rory again. Maybe he got off work early. They could go to National or even a local dive like the Pig & Duke. But it wasn't Rory.

— Amy: Are you back in town?

Drew looked at the message still visible on the locked screen. If he entered his password, the app would open and she would see that he had read the message. He looked up and stared at the game blankly, thinking of what to do. *Pacioretty in for the face-off, Tavares wins it cleanly, passes to Johnston who has room to skate the puck into the Montréal zone. Jordan Eberle on the forecheck, takes the puck away, gets into the high slot and stopped by Price who shuts the door on Eberle.*

Fuck it.

— Drew: Yeah just got back. Go for a drink?
— Amy: Sure... Tin Palace?
— Drew: K yeah, meet you in fifteen. Gotta get
               gas for the truck.

Drew wrestled with his decision as he put on a collared shirt and brushed his hair. He should have shaved but, whatever. She always liked the rustic look. Yeah and she's going to think you're getting back together. So, what? Maybe we should get back together. It was stupid we broke up in the first place. She's gonna be pissed that you're going boarding tomorrow. Yeah, well, maybe she can come — okay she doesn't ski, and Rory will be pissed, but Rory is always pissed at something. He'll probably bail anyway. His boss always wants him to work weekends. Drew grabbed his wallet and his keys, checking over his appearance one last time. He paused just before turning off the television.

And there's Shea Weber, right on cue, able to put it home on the power play. You know he has been having a rough start to the season, only thirteen points — but what a textbook goal from the veteran player.

ACKNOWLEDGEMENTS

Thank you for picking up the second edition of A Rough Season, originally published by Loft on EIGHTH Press in Calgary. I originally wrote this story at the University of Edinburgh in 2018. I tried to write the most Canadian, and Calgarian, story I could think of. So much of my writing career is owed to the University of Edinburgh including; Jane, RAJ, Claire and my brilliant friends in workshop B. Thank you to Ryan, Sam, Sonali, Huriyah, Lis, Chelsea, Paige, Christa, Tommi and David, who heard this one first. This story wouldn't be possible without my friends and family for supporting me in my writing journey. For 17th Avenue; you keep Calgary who we are.

ABOUT THE AUTHOR

L.L. Angelo is a professional writer and author. She holds a Master's with Distinction in Creative Writing from The University of Edinburgh and a Bachelor of Arts from Royal Roads University. She is the recipient of the Carlyle Norman Scholarship for Emerging Literary Artists Endowment, and was awarded a residency at The Banff Centre with award-winning writer Ayelet Tsabari. Her chapbook titled *A Rough Season* was first released in 2020 by Loft on Eighth Press. She has been published in anthologies including: *From Arthur's Seat 3* by Egg Box Publishing (UK) and *The War Memory Project* by the Alexandra Writer's Centre in Canada. She is a member of the Writer's Union of Canada, Society of Young Publishers and Society of Authors. Her work has also appeared in Culinaire Magazine, Neon Magazine, 5 on the Fifth and The Flexible Persona Magazine.

L.L. Angelo teaches writing at the University of Calgary and Mount Royal University.

Follow her on twitter @angelolexie

For news and events, visit www.lexieangelo.com

SPECIAL THANKS

Loft 112

Villiage Brewery

Calgary Arts Development

University of Edinburgh

University of Calgary

Mount Royal University

Calgary Public Library

IngramSpark